Dear Maria

Happy 4th Birthday

Love & Kisses

Grandma Maria

Miss Tizzy

Miss Tizzy

By Libba Moore Gray
Illustrated by Jada Rowland

Simon & Schuster Books for Young Readers

Miss Tizzy always wore a purple hat with a white flower in it and high-top green tennis shoes. The neighbors thought her peculiar. But the children loved her.

Miss Tizzy's house was pink and sat like a fat blossom in the middle of a street with white houses, white fences, and very neat flower gardens. Miss Tizzy had no fence at all but she had flowers that grew everywhere and spilled over onto the sidewalk.

Miss Tizzy let the children pick the flowers. Then she gave them clean glass jelly jars to put them in. And the children loved it.

Miss Tizzy's big, yellow cat, Hiram, slept in a window box in the middle of some red geraniums. Sometimes he climbed on her shoulders and hung there like a tired old fur piece.

RICE
TEA

On Mondays, Miss Tizzy baked cookies. She let the neighborhood children put in the raisins, and then lick the bowl while the cookies were baking. The children loved it.

On Tuesdays, Miss Tizzy made puppets out of old socks. She made a puppet for each boy and girl. They made up their own stories and put on shows for Miss Tizzy. She laughed and clapped every time. And the children loved it.

On Wednesdays, Miss Tizzy played her bagpipes. She gave the children spoons and pans and let them pretend they were playing real drums. Each Wednesday, one child got to be special and play a

silver penny whistle. Every child got a turn. They marched up and down the street with Miss Tizzy and her bagpipes leading the parade. Hiram sometimes marched along, and the children loved it.

On Thursdays, Miss Tizzy gave the children clean, white paper and crayons. They drew pictures of sunshine and butterflies. They put them in Miss Tizzy's red wagon and delivered them all over town to people who had stopped smiling, and had grown too tired to come out of their houses anymore. Hiram rode in the front of the wagon with a red ribbon around his neck. And the children loved it.

On Fridays, Miss Tizzy opened her trunk and they all played dress up. There were hats with feathers and hats with bows. There were baseball caps and straw hats with bright, red bands. Everyone wore a hat. Miss Tizzy put on a lace shawl and served pink lemonade in her best china cups. The children loved it.

On Saturdays, Miss Tizzy put roller skates on her green tennis shoes and went up and down the sidewalks. The children came out of the white houses and joined her. They made a roller-skate train holding on to Miss Tizzy's long skirt. Hiram was usually the caboose. The children made train sounds and Miss Tizzy was the engineer. She never scolded the children for being too loud, and the children loved it.

On Sundays, when the day was over, the children stretched out on bright quilts in Miss Tizzy's backyard and looked up at the stars. The tree frogs croaked their summer sounds as Miss Tizzy sang songs about the moon, slightly off-key. The children didn't care. They loved it.

One day Miss Tizzy took off her purple hat with the white flower and laid it on the window seat. Then she took off her high-top green tennis shoes and placed them under her high white bed. Miss Tizzy lay down on her feather mattress. She was very sick. Hiram left his window box and curled up at her feet. He did not purr anymore. The doctor came and went. He shook his head and looked very serious.

The children were sad. They didn't know what to do. They missed their grown-up friend. Finally.... they had an idea.

On Monday, they baked cookies with raisins and brought them to the pink house.

On Tuesday, they stood in the yard and held up puppets to the window. They put on a puppet show just for Miss Tizzy.

On Wednesday, they brought pans and spoons and played a soft little drumming sound just outside the door.

On Thursday, they drew pictures with orange and red crayons and put them in Miss Tizzy's mailbox.

On Friday, they put on funny hats and left a tea tray at the front door. They left Hiram a bowl of cool milk.

On Saturday, they put a brand new pair of skates in a big box with a purple ribbon on top and took them to Miss Tizzy.

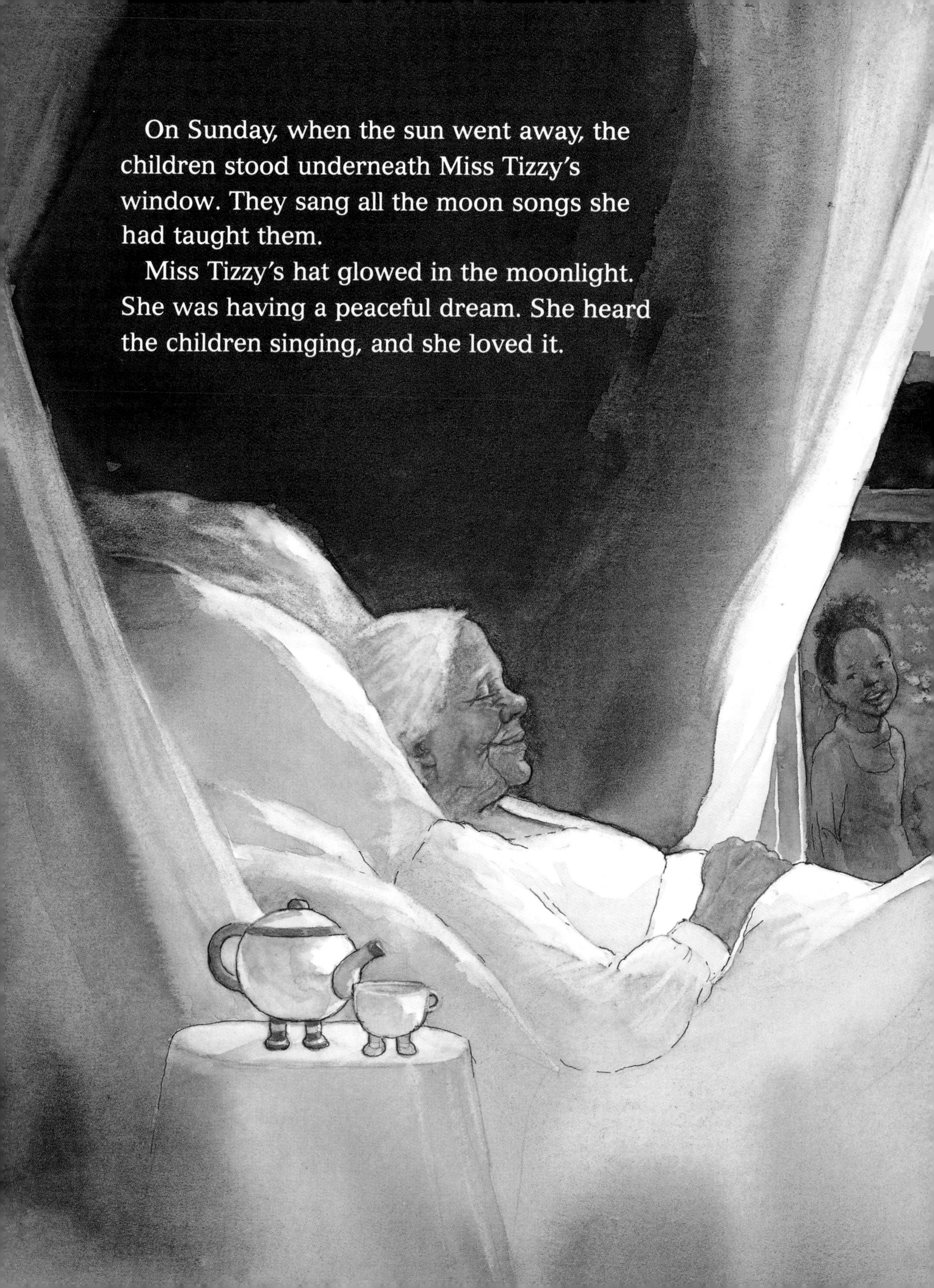

On Sunday, when the sun went away, the children stood underneath Miss Tizzy's window. They sang all the moon songs she had taught them.

Miss Tizzy's hat glowed in the moonlight. She was having a peaceful dream. She heard the children singing, and she loved it.

For my family and students
and in memory of Alex Todd Fleming
and Anne Moorhead Segars
— L.M.G.

To my nieces:
Debran, Anastasia and Ariadne
— J.R.

SIMON & SCHUSTER BOOKS FOR YOUNG READERS
An imprint of Simon & Schuster Children's Publishing Division
1230 Avenue of the Americas
New York, New York 10020

The text of this book is set in 14pt. Versailles 55.
The illustrations were done in watercolor, pen and ink.
Designed by Vicki Kalajian.
Manufactured in the United States of America

10 9 8 7

Library of Congress Cataloging-in-Publication Data
Gray, Libba Moore. Miss Tizzy / by Libba Moore Gray ;
illustrated by Jada Rowland.
p. cm. Summary: The eccentric Miss Tizzy, a beloved friend
to all the children in her neighborhood,
needs their help in remaining happy when she is sick in bed.
[1. Individuality—Fiction. 2. Sick—Fiction.]
I. Rowland, Jada, ill. II. Title.
PZ7.G7793Mi 1993 [E]—dc20 92-8409 CIP AC
ISBN: 0-671-77590-1